DIYA DANCES THE DANDIYA

Written by
PRIA DEE

Illustrated by
YOUNGJU KIM

Dedicated:

To all those who enjoy
dance and music

Diya was backstage, waiting for her turn to dance. Just three more acts before her group's performance at the annual Navaratri celebrations. She had looked forward to it for weeks and weeks.

Her sister, Sita, called for everyone to get into costume. She was the choreographer for Diya's dance.

Diya couldn't stop smiling as she dressed in her pretty, pink lehenga and green choli blouse. Next, the jhumka earrings that looked like church bells and her favorite silver anklets.

Wait! Where were her anklets?

She wore them earlier that day for the dress rehearsal on stage. The anklets were an important part of her costume, the tiny bells tinkling in rhythm to the music as she danced. She couldn't perform without them!

Diya ran to her mom, who was setting up stage decorations for the next group.

"Have you seen my anklets, Amma?" she asked.

Amma shook her head. She hadn't seen them.

"Never mind!" Diya shouted. She ran away faster than a bunny before Amma could ask any questions.

In her hurry, she tripped over her little brother, Ramu, who watched her curiously. He was dressed in his kurta and pajamas.

"Have you seen my anklets, Ramu?" she asked.

"No! No! No!" said Ramu, wagging his finger, not helpful at all.

Diya squeezed her eyes and screwed up her face, trying to remember where she had last seen them.

Aha! They must be in the green room!

She raced to the green room with Ramu at her heels.

Diya found her dance sticks on the table. Sita was applying kajal to her eyes in front of the mirror. Ramu ran over to give her a kiss.

"Have you seen my anklets, Sita?" Diya asked, peeking into the mirror.

Sita shook her head as she fixed a red bindi on her forehead. She had not seen them.

"Where did I go next?" Diya wondered. "I know! We ate samosas in the dining room after the rehearsal." She raced to the dining room, interrupting a group of moms who were setting up snacks and chai.

No anklets! But Diva found her green dupatta and a half-eaten samosa on a table. Ramu helped himself to the samosa with a gap-toothed grin.

"Tara and I were playing backstage earlier. Maybe she knows where they are," she told Ramu.

Diya dashed backstage. She found Tara there, fully dressed in her costume.

"Have you seen my anklets, Tara?" she asked hopefully.

Tara lifted her skirt to show off her own anklets and shook her head.

Ramu peeked under all the props and supplies behind the stage. No anklets, but he did find a box of laddu that he inspected with glee.

"Did you check the washroom?" Tara asked.

"That's right. I washed my hands after the samosa!" Diya said, rushing off. Ramu trotted next to her with a laddu in each hand.

In the restroom, Diva found her golden bangles on the counter, but no anklets!

"I need the bangles for the dance, too, but where could my anklets be?" She slipped on the bangles.

Ramu sat on the counter, gobbling his laddu, and shook his head.

"Diya, I've been looking for you!" Sita exclaimed, entering the restroom. "You should be dressed by now." She lifted Ramu down and brushed off the laddu crumbs.

"I can't find my anklets!" Diya sobbed. "Can you help me?"

Sita nodded.

They searched everywhere, and Diva's dance group helped. They looked under the dining room tables, beneath the auditorium chairs, and even behind the curtains on stage. It was almost time for the performance, but still no anklets!

Crestfallen, and with tears bright in her eyes, Diya returned to the dressing room dragging her feet. She could not dance after all. Not without her anklets! She would ask Amma to take her home. Her pretty dance lehenga made her feel like a princess, but now no one would see her dancing in it.

She sighed and pulled out her coat. The coat jingled, but Diya was too sad to notice. She shrugged into a sleeve. The coat jangled! This time, Diya heard it. She gasped and her eyes lit up. She dug her hands into her pockets and pulled out first one, then the other anklet!

"They were here all the time!" she shouted, jumping up and down. "I put them in my coat pocket to keep them safe!"

Sita helped Diya drape the dupatta around her and fastened the anklets around her ankles. They tinkled merrily with her steps. When Diya picked up the dance sticks, she looked like a princess indeed!

Ramu sat nearby, scribbling lipstick over the mirror.

Sita led Diya and her group onto the stage. A cheerful song played in Hindi.

On cue, Diya and the other children clicked their sticks in rhythm as they danced the Dandiya, skipping and moving in a circle. It was so much fun!

When it was over, Diya carefully placed her entire costume with her anklets in a big box in the closet to keep it safe for next time.

And that night she dreamed that she was a princess with tiny bells on, dancing the Dandiya.

THE END

Hindi Glossary - Names

Diya: lamp or light

Tara: star

Sita: garden

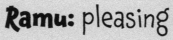

Ramu: pleasing

Clothes

Jhumka earrings: bell-shaped earrings

Dupatta: scarf

Choli: blouse

Lehenga: long skirt

Bindi: beauty spot on forehead worn by girls

Kurta: tunic shirt

Sari: a traditional garment worn by adults. 5-yard fabric pleated and draped over an underskirt

Pajama: pants

Hindi Glossary - Culture

Navaratri: Festival of Nine Nights to overcome evil with good

Dandiya: traditional dance during Navaratri festival. Danced by clicking sticks together

Hindi: the language spoken in large areas of northern and western India

Hindi Glossary - Food

Laddu: yellow sweet made with chickpea flour and syrup

Samosa: pastry stuffed with vegetables and fried

Chai: tea with milk

Lightning Source UK Ltd.
Milton Keynes UK
UKHW051507040922
408168UK00002BA/48